Who is Liverpool's Prettiest Princess?

DISCOVER MORE OF YOUR TOWN
HOMETOWN WORLD

Written by Rachel Elliot
Illustrated by Annabel Spenceley

Everyone in the palace is very excited.
The handsome prince is hosting
a Grand Ball. He has written
lots of golden invitations.

Dear ....

Everyone keeps telling me to marry a princess. But I don't want to marry a princess! I want to marry my one true love. I will think she is the prettiest and loveliest girl in Liverpool. I'm holding a Grand Ball at Liverpool Town Hall so that I can meet her and dance with her.

I hope you can come!

The Prince

There is just one question on everyone's lips...

Who is the prince going to choose?

The handsome prince sends his littlest courtier to deliver invitations to all the girls in Liverpool.

The littlest courtier walks along tree-lined streets. He walks through busy squares and grassy parks. Everywhere he goes, he asks the same question.

"Who do *you* think is the loveliest girl in Liverpool?"

The littlest courtier asks the children visiting St George's Hall. "Holly has the **sweetest** smile," says a little girl.

Holly is full of **fun**.
She lives in a castle on
Lord Street.

She has tumbling
golden curls and big
blue eyes, and she loves
dressing up best of all.

When the littlest courtier
gives her the golden invitation,
she smiles sweetly
and does

cartwheels

all around the castle!

Holly is very excited to be invited to the ball. She goes to Bold Street to buy a new dress.

"Who will the prince dance with tonight?" asks the dressmaker.

"I hope he chooses me," says Holly. "My new dress will

float

across the floor as we dance."

The littlest courtier meets an old gardener in Stanley Park.

"Who do you think is the loveliest girl in Liverpool?" he asks.

"Rani has the kindest eyes," says the old gardener.

Rani is very graceful. She lives in a grand house on Duke Street. She has thick brown ringlets and sparkling hazel eyes, and she loves dancing best of all.

Ding dong!

The littlest courtier rings the clanging doorbell and gives Rani the invitation. Her eyes twinkle kindly.

Rani can't wait for the ball to start! She goes to
Clayton Square to buy a new pair of dancing shoes.

"Who will the
prince dance
with tonight?"

asks the shoemaker.

"I hope he chooses me," says Rani. "I'll dance until my new shoes are

worn out!"

Tip tap! Tippety tap!

The littlest courtier meets a clown doing magic tricks in Concert Square.

"Who do you think is the loveliest girl in Liverpool?" he asks.

"Sophia has the cutest giggle," says the clown.

Sophia is very gentle. She lives in a house at the top of Everton Hill, and she loves **SEQUINS** best of all.

She has a **shiny** black bob and **glimmering brown** eyes.

Sophia giggles in excitement as the littlest courtier gives her the golden invitation.

Sophia goes to Cavern Walks and buys a sequinned headband.

It sparkles gold and silver.

"Who will the prince dance with tonight?"

asks the jeweller.

"I hope he chooses me," says Sophia. "My headband will glitter under the

chandeliers!"

The courtier meets a chimney sweep in Wavertree.

"Who do you think is the loveliest girl in Liverpool?" he asks.

"Chloe has the most enchanting voice," says the chimney sweep.

Chloe lives in a pretty cottage in Knotty Ash, and she loves MUSIC best of all.

She has big bouncy curls and deep brown eyes. When the littlest courtier gives Chloe her invitation, she sings happily.

The littlest courtier runs around Liverpool all day long. From Aintree to Anfield, from Bootle to Otterspool, from Sefton Park to Stanley Park and everywhere in between, he makes sure that every girl is invited.

The littlest courtier delivers his last invitation just as the sun is beginning to set. Feeling tired but content, he turns and walks back to the palace.

The sun sets and the moon and stars start to glimmer.

Lots of girls arrive outside Liverpool Town Hall.

The street is filled with the sound of laughter.

Dresses are rustling.

Sequins are sparkling.

It's time for the ball to start!

Inside the Town Hall there is a spotless shiny dance floor.

The band is playing **beautiful** music.

The chandeliers are **shimmering** in the candlelight.

The handsome prince sits on his golden throne,
watching his guests arrive. Everyone is very excited!
They are all wondering one thing...

Who will he
choose?

The prince walks through the crowd, talking
to each of his guests in turn. Finally, he holds out
his hand to one of the girls. "You are the prettiest
and loveliest girl in all of Liverpool," he says.

The handsome prince dances with his one
true love. He will marry her and make her
a princess!

But **WHO IS** his chosen princess?

It's YOU!